A Birthday for Bear

Bonny Becker

illustrated by

Kady MacDonald Denton

CANDLEWICK PRESS

For Kurt, who celebrates
B. B.

To Sally
K. D.

Text copyright © 2009 by Bonny Becker
Illustrations copyright © 2009 by Kady MacDonald Denton

First paperback edition in this format 2013

The Library of Congress has cataloged the hardcover edition as follows:

Becker, Bonny.
A Birthday for Bear / Bonny Becker ;
illustrated by Kady MacDonald Denton. — 1st ed.
p. cm.
Summary: Despite Bear's efforts to ignore his birthday,
Mouse will not rest until his friend celebrates.
ISBN 978-0-7636-3746-0 (hardcover)
[1. Birthdays—Fiction. 2. Bears—Fiction. 3. Mice—Fiction. 4. Friendship—Fiction.]
I. Denton, Kady MacDonald, ill. II. Title.
PZ7.B3814Bi 2009
[E]—dc22   2008021412

ISBN 978-0-7636-6861-7 (paperback)

17 18 SWT 10 9 8 7 6 5

Printed in Dongguan, Guangdong, China

This book was typeset in New Baskerville.
The illustrations were done in ink and watercolor.

Candlewick Press
99 Dover Street
Somerville, Massachusetts 02144

visit us at www.candlewick.com

CONTENTS

Bear didn't like birthdays.

He didn't like birthday parties or balloons.

He didn't like birthday cards or songs or candles.

In fact, Bear was quite sure he didn't like

anything to do with birthdays at all.

Chapter 1

Swish! Swish! Swish! Bear dusted his shelves.

Whisk! Whisk! Whisk! Bear swept his floor.

He was very, very busy today. Bear was always

very, very busy on his birthday.

He opened the door to shake out his broom, and there was Mouse, small and gray and bright-eyed.

"Happy birthday, Bear!" cried Mouse.

"It's not my birthday," lied Bear.

"But it says so right here," said Mouse, waving a party invitation.

"Let me see that!" demanded Bear. He peered at the card. It read:

Dear Mouse,
Come to Bear's birthday
at Bear's house today!
Balloons and presents
and birthday cake.

"This is your handwriting!" protested Bear. "*You* wrote it."

"Did I?" asked Mouse, most innocently.

"Yes," said Bear. He sounded quite certain.

Mouse hung his head. "Shameful trickery," he confessed. "Terribly sorry. But perhaps we could have just a little birthday party?"

"I do not like parties. I do not like birthdays. And I especially do not like birthday parties for me at my house," Bear announced, and he swept Mouse out the door.

Chapter 2

Slop! Slop! Slop! Bear mopped the hallway.

He heard a tap, tap, tapping on his back door.

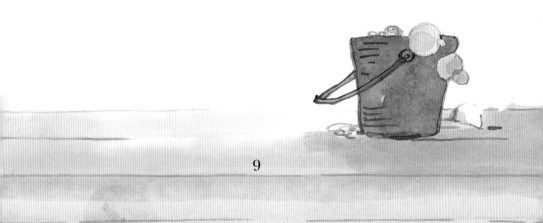

He opened the door, and there stood a tiny
deliveryman holding three red balloons.

"Happy Birthday balloons for a
Mr. Bear," announced the deliveryman.

Bear narrowed his eyes.

"You are not a deliveryman. You are Mouse! I can see your tail," declared Bear, pointing an accusing claw.

Mouse hung his head. "Deepest apologies," he said. "But surely you would like just one balloon? It bats about quite nicely."

"I do not like balloons. I do not like parties. And I do not like birthdays," said Bear. He shut the door with a firm bang.

13

Slosh! Slosh! Slosh! Bear scrubbed the counters and washed the dishes.

He heard a rap, rap, rapping on his kitchen window.

Bear opened his window.

There stood a little postman holding a
bright red envelope.

"A Birthday Greeting for Bear," said the postman, reading the envelope.

Bear crossed his arms.

"You are not the postman. You are

Mouse!" cried Bear. "I can see your ears."

"Appalling behavior—" Mouse started
to say, but Bear slammed the window shut.

Chapter 3

Squidjedy! Squidjedy! Squidjedy! Bear polished his living-room clock. What a very, very busy day he was having.

Bear pricked up his ears. There was a scritch, scritch, scratching sound coming from his fireplace.

Onto the hearth bounced a tiny
Santa Claus!

"Ho, ho, ho!" cried the little Santa
Claus. "A Christmas present for Bear!"

Christmas already? thought Bear. He reached for the present, then snatched back his paw.

"Wait a minute," growled Bear. "It's not Christmas. It's my birthday!"

"You said it *wasn't* your birthday!" The little Santa looked very pleased with himself.

Bear glared.

"Well, you are not Santa," he shouted.

"You are Mouse. I can see your whiskers!"

"Ah, you are too clever for me, Bear," Mouse admitted. "But, still, you must like birthday presents. Everyone likes a present."

Bear pulled himself up to his full height
and roared,

"I do not like presents.
I do not like birthday cards.
I do not like balloons.
I do not like parties.
I do not like BIRTHDAYS!"

"And look! You've scattered ashes all over my nice clean hearth!" Bear trembled with anger. "I am very, very, VERY busy today!"

"It's quite a lovely present," Mouse said, and he sadly dragged it away.

Chapter 4

Bear wiped up the ashes from the hearth. The hearth was shiny and clean. No mouse prints. Good!

Bear swept up the ashes on the floor and whisked them out the back door. Mouse and the messy present were gone. Hurrah!

Squeak! Squeak! Squeak! Bear scrubbed
his windows. No Mouse in sight. Yes!

Bear's paw slowed to a stop. Bear stared
out the window. No one had ever given Bear
a present before.

Bear swallowed. He had noticed that it was an especially big present, too. He wondered what sort of especially big present it might be.

Ding-dong went the doorbell.

Bear opened the door. There on the stoop was a pink box.

"You don't fool me, Mouse! I know you're in there!" Bear cried, springing open the lid of the box.

But inside was just a cake. A big cake with chocolate sprinkles and the words *Happy Birthday, Bear* in chocolate icing.

"I do not like birthday cake, either!"
Bear announced loudly so that Mouse could
hear.

Bear glared into the bushes, looked
behind the door, and peeked under the box.
No postmen, no deliverymen, no Santas.
No Mouse.

Bear picked up the box and hurried to
the kitchen.

Bear glanced around, then lifted out the cake. He swiped a pawful of creamy icing and was just about to plop it in his mouth, when—

Out of the cake popped Mouse! Small and gray and bright-eyed!

"A-haa!" cried Mouse. "You *do* like birthday cake!"

Bear looked down at the chocolate cake with chocolate icing and chocolate sprinkles.

"I made it myself," added Mouse with
an eager flick of his tail.

No one had ever made Bear a birthday
cake before.

Even so, Bear started to say, "I am very,
very busy today," but then he didn't.

"Chocolate is my favorite," Bear admitted.

Mouse flicked his tail and whisked out the door.

"Wait!" Bear cried.

Quick as a whisker, Mouse was back. He tied three red balloons to Bear's chair, plunked a sparkly birthday hat on Bear's head, and set the especially big present on Bear's lap.

Bear lifted the lid from his present.
Crickle. Crackle. Crinkle. He parted the crisp
white paper.

In the box nestled a pair of shiny red roller skates—just the right size for a bear.

"Happy birthday!" cried Mouse.

"Thank you, Mouse," said Bear gruffly. "I've always wanted a pair of shiny red roller skates." Bear cleared his throat. "Perhaps I don't mind birthdays after all."

Then Bear cut a big slice of cake for himself and an especially big slice for Mouse.

And Bear and Mouse ate the whole cake—every sprinkle and crumb.